POMPEII

Carmel Reilly

Australia • Brazil • Japan • Korea • Mexico • Singapore • Spain • United Kingdom • United States

Pompeii

Fast Forward
Purple Level 19

Text: Carmel Reilly
Illustrations: Boris Silvestri
Editor: Johanna Rohan
Designer: Stella Vassiliou
Series designer: James Lowe
Production controller: Seona Galbally
Photo research: Michelle Cottrill
Audio recordings: Juliet Hill, Picture Start
Spoken by: Matthew King and Abbe Holmes
Reprint: Siew Han Ong

Acknowledgements
The author and publisher would like to acknowledge permission to reproduce material from the following sources: Photographs from AGEFotostock/ Peter Phipp, p. 21 bottom; Getty Images/ National Geographic, p. 4/ PhotoDisc, p. 8 left; Photolibrary/ Carrasco Demetrio, front cover top, pp. 1 top, 21 top/ SPL/ David A. Hardy, p. 8 right/ Jeremy Bishop, p. 10 bottom/ JTB Photo, p. 20 top/ SPL, back cover, p. 9/ The Bridgeman Art Library, pp. 19 top, 18-19/ Tony Craddock, p. 20 bottom/ Vincent Leblic, front cover bottom, pp. 1 bottom, 23 top/ Alamy/ North Wind Picture Archives, p. 11 top; The Art Archive/ Archaeological Museum Naples/ Dagli Orti (A), p. 23 bottom/ Bibliotheque Paris/ Marc Charmet, p. 11 bottom/ Dagli Orti, p. 22.

ISBN 978 0 17 012652 6
ISBN 978 0 17 012645 8 (set)

Cengage Learning Australia
Level 7, 80 Dorcas Street
South Melbourne, Victoria Australia 3205
Phone: 1300 790 853

Cengage Learning New Zealand
Unit 4B Rosedale Office Park
331 Rosedale Road, Albany, North Shore NZ 0632
Phone: 0800 449 725

For learning solutions, visit **cengage.com.au**

Printed in China by 1010 Printing International Ltd
6 7 8 9 15

Evaluated in independent research by staff from the Department of Language, Literacy and Arts Education at the University of Melbourne.

Carmel Reilly

Contents

Chapter 1

24 AUGUST, 79 AD

The city of Pompeii was a part of the **Roman Empire**, in the first century AD.

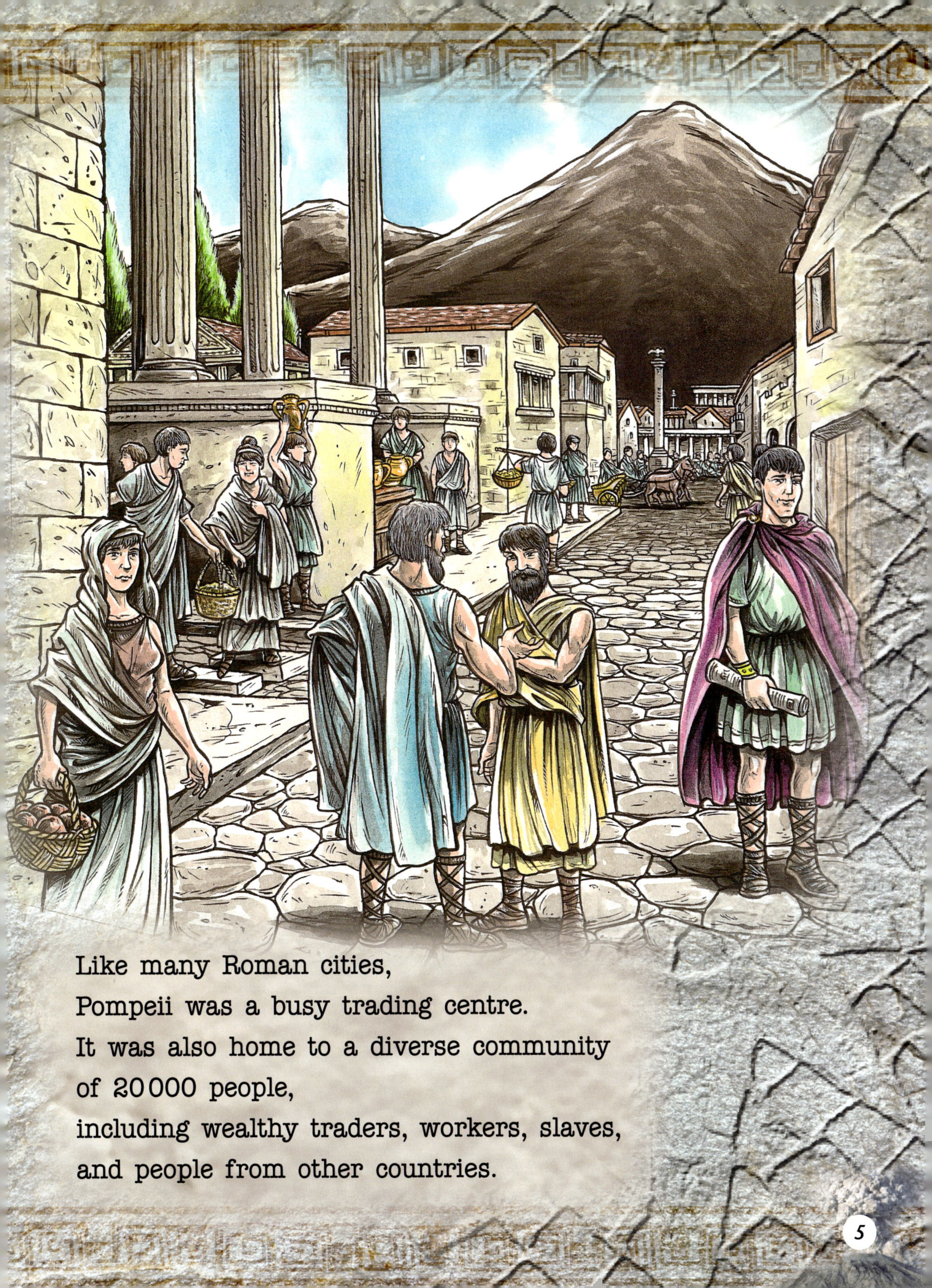

Like many Roman cities,
Pompeii was a busy trading centre.
It was also home to a diverse community
of 20 000 people,
including wealthy traders, workers, slaves,
and people from other countries.

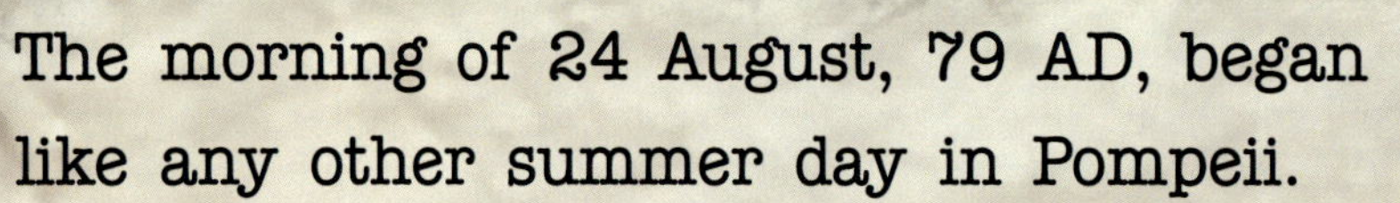

The morning of 24 August, 79 AD, began like any other summer day in Pompeii.

People were up and about
before the Sun rose.
In the homes of the wealthy,
slaves made breakfast for their owners.
In the homes of the poor,
people made their own breakfast of porridge
before going to work.

By sunrise, Pompeii's streets were busy.
Farmers made their way to the market
to sell food.
Women and slaves got water at the wells.
In the **forum**, shops, government buildings,
temples and the baths
were open for business.
At school, children began their lessons.

Chapter 2

THE ERUPTION

It was just after sunrise
when the people of Pompeii
felt the first earthquakes.
The earthquakes were followed by
great flashes of light shooting from the top
of Mount Vesuvius –
only a few kilometres away.

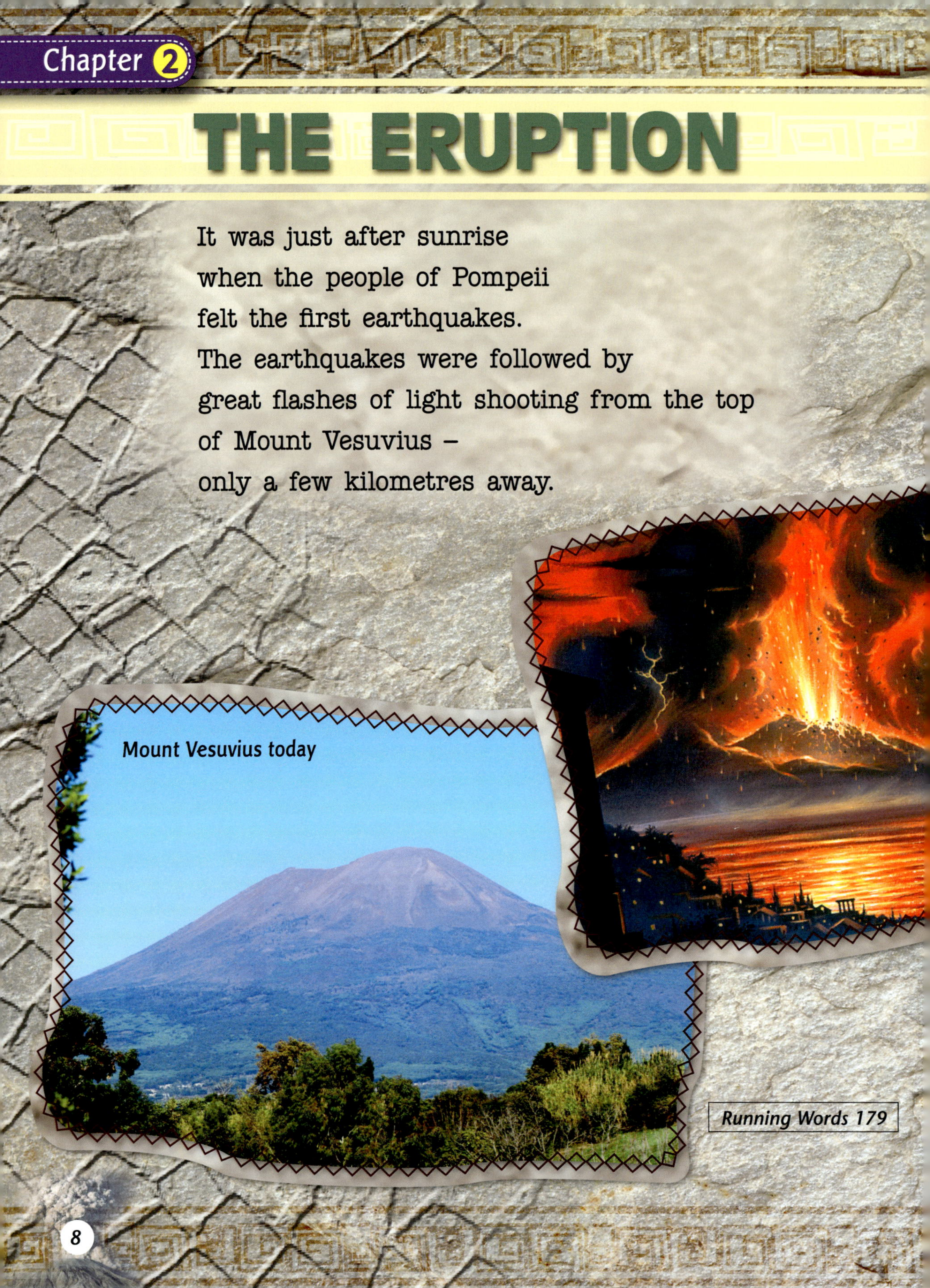

Mount Vesuvius today

Running Words 179

Soon after, hot ash and rocks
began to rain down on the city.
The sky grew dark as the ash blocked out the Sun.

Within a short time, the sky was black. The air was hot and full of the sounds of the volcano.

Fires broke out all over the city.
The hot rocks hit the wooden parts of the houses and the houses caught alight.
Then, thick ash began to fall, covering everything, including people, animals and buildings.

Chapter 3

ESCAPE

The people of Pompeii began to panic.
They pushed their way through the narrow streets, trying to escape from the city.

Although it was dark,
the fires and the flashes from the eruption
gave them a little light to see.
Some people were lucky –
they reached the city gates quickly
and left by road.

Chapter 4

WAITING

Other people ran to the nearby beach in the hope of leaving by boat. But, they found that the sea was wild, and the earthquakes had pushed the tide out. Not wanting to go back into Pompeii, most people decided to wait where they were.

Within the walls of Pompeii,
many people had taken their families and slaves
into their houses' basements.
They thought they would be safe there
until the eruption was over.

Poisonous gases were now seeping out of Mount Vesuvius. Within a few minutes, the gases drifted across the city and down to the beach, killing everything.

The ash kept falling.
It made its way inside houses and into basements.
It covered the bodies of the dead
and slowly buried the city.

Chapter 5

BURIED

When the eruption stopped
and the ash cooled down,
the survivors returned to Pompeii.
Pompeii was covered
in layers of volcanic ash and rock,
and only the tops of a few buildings could be seen.
In just one day, the community of Pompeii
had been wiped out.

Although a few people dug up treasures,
Pompeii was left mostly untouched.
Over the years, grass and trees grew over the site
and the city disappeared.

Chapter 6

DISCOVERED RUINS

Pompeii was not discovered again until the 1700s. A farmer found ruins of the city under his land. Since then, most of the city has been uncovered, and now thousands of people visit Pompeii each year.

The city is well preserved
because it was buried under ash.
Visitors to Pompeii today can walk along the streets
and see art and graffiti on the walls of the buildings,
just as it was on the day of the eruption.

Visitors can see plaster models
of people who died in the eruption,
in the museum.
Visitors can also see the everyday things
these people used,
and even the remains of some of their food.

Many people have mixed feelings when they visit Pompeii. On one hand, it is interesting to see what life was like in an ancient Roman community.
But, on the other hand, the place is a sad reminder of the thousands of lives that ended suddenly so long ago.

Glossary

forum a large town square

Roman Empire the empire under Roman rule established in 27 BC

Index